A MOTHER'S PAIN

Deivone M. Tanksley Sr.

Edited by Everton Russell Jr

authorHOUSE®

AuthorHouse™ LLC
1663 Liberty Drive
Bloomington, IN 47403
www.authorhouse.com
Phone: 1-800-839-8640

Published by AuthorHouse   12/07/2013

ISBN: 978-1-4918-4050-4 (sc)
ISBN: 978-1-4918-4051-1 (hc)
ISBN: 978-1-4918-4052-8 (e)

Library of Congress Control Number: 2013921876

Illustrator Info: Emanuel Morell, Mannymanson4@gmail.com

CONTENTS

(SHE IS)

She is...
what beauty is..,
And always was...
Suppose to be,
Her..
Ebony tone!,
Has Glown!,
all across the sea's!,
Skin full of melanin..
so soft, so strong,
a color in which the sun has forged a bond!..
Yet..
beaten and battered!,
what comes from her through birth..
which is my earth!
my D.N.A mastered!..
I am here for mine!
she will not!..
Birth a bastard!..
Worked these lands..
blood sweat and tears,
even running for freedom like a bandit..
So a peace of this American pie for her..
hope you don't mind if I..
just grab it!..

Place my queen on that pedestal..
It's her birth right! to live lavish!
But this does come at cost My queen!..
See..
I have baggage!..
Insecurities, subliminal plights..
In a nation where my struggle is far from light,
Guiding is she to my darkness!,
land bound!
as I a ship lost at sea embrace her guiding lite
so I may find my way home..
She is my foundation..
My Mt rush more..
may I..
rush ashore!
back too the essence of that I adorn..
My seed my creation!
she takes incubating!
9months till the sac called home is torn!..
A mothers pain is where...
love is born!!!

Written by:
Everton A Russell jr.
Erussell860@gmail.com
(CEO) "Russell Imagery Photography"
R.imagery@gmail.com

CHAPTER 1

Suddenly, he races outside, jumps into his car, slams his foot on the gas causing his tires to burn out, speed begins to pick up very fast, swerving in and out of traffic, one hand on the wheel[the other rubbing his head] music blasting loud! One hundred, one hundred and ten, one hundred and twenty miles per hour, car starts to shake, hard to control tears pouring down his face. But wait a minute. In order for you to understand this story, we have to start way back from the very beginning.

There was a strong black women by the name of Crystal. When I say strong, I mean strong, physically and mentally. She was a good women, very attractive, stood about five foot eight, dark brown hair, big brown eyes and nice lips and a beautiful body with perfect curves. On a hot sunny day the only thing you can think about is your lips all over her beautiful body. Crystal was always working, she was a RN. She worked days, nights and double shifts. She did everything she had to do to keep her children housed, clothed, and fed. Being a single mom was not easy at all. It was like a full time job, but the only difference was, she didn't receive a pay check at the end of the week. Instead, she received a lot of pain and suffering. Crystal was constantly stressing over bills, tired and exhausted, almost feeling as if she was ready to give up. Then that unconditional love would kick right back in giving her that boost she needs to keep on going. That's why she was so powerful.

Crystal wasn't always a single mom she was left with a remembrance in her head that would never go away.

One night, her husband Ronny took her out for their fifth year anniversary to a fancy restaurant overlooking the city. It was a perfect night. The moon was at its fullest, the sky was filled with stars so big and bright. Their table was decorated with beautiful pink and white flowers, five candles lit, one for each year along with a bottle of expensive wine to go with their meal. If anybody knew how to treat a women it would have been him. After dinner and sharing a moist piece of chocolate raspberry cake for dessert, her favorite, he leaned over the table and slowly kissed his beautiful wife on the lips. They made a toast saying, "to what the future holds." After leaving the restaurant on their way home, he played a song by John Legend, "You and I." He looks over to his wife and before he can tell her how much he loves her, a suv comes out of nowhere, crashing into them causing their car to flip over three, or four times. Pieces of metal and shattered glass flying everywhere.

The car then came to a stop after smashing into a telephone pole, smoke coming from the hood. Ronny and Crystal were both stuck. Crystal was able to squeeze out of the window and crawled to the driver's side to find Ronny unconscious and starts to shake and pull on him but nothing. She's so weak and he still wasn't responding. She then starts to speak to him in a crying voice. "Come on baby, please wake up we have to get out of here!" Crystal then notice flames from the corner of her eye. She became paranoid and started to scream and pull, scream and pull and pulled until she passed out. Ronny then gains consciousness and struggles to get out and look for his wife. He finds her laying in the street right outside his door. He picks Crystal up, putting her over his shoulder and begins to walk, he walked for almost a mile before he collapsed. They both were later found then rushed to the ER. Ronny later died. The doctor said he wasn't only a hero for his wife but also for his children whose date of birth matched the date he died. Yes, that night Crystal gave birth to a set of twin boys and named them Ronny and Johnny.

CHAPTER 2

Both boys favored their dad very much. Especially Ronny Jr. from his looks to his attitude, you name it he had it, Ronny was the spitting image of his dad. He was about six feet tall, real slim, brown skin and always kept a fresh haircut no matter what. He was athletic, very intelligent, respectful, and consistent in everything he did. For a fourteen year old kid at that time becoming a professional ball player was something that every kid dream of, but not for him, it was more like a hobby. Ronny always thought a little bit different than most of his friends. He was motivated and determined to reach his biggest goal and that was ownership. Just his form of thinking was so powerful, things like making investments, starting his own business, maintaining ownership and more. He might have been young but he had an old soul. "Think big"- "Hit big" was his M.O. Ronny spent a lot of time reading and increasing his knowledge. He would read books like, The Science of Getting Rich, Black Girl Lost, Ponder on This, Malcom X, Roots, and many more. He wasn't into too much music, but he did admire one artist by the name of Shawn Carter {some might know him as Jay Z} but for him, the CDs weren't just CDs. They were more like art, true advice over smooth beats. So he would study them.

Jonny on the other hand was the youngest but only by a few minutes. He also was about six feet tall, brown skin, and very slim. Johnny was more of a pretty boy type. He was a fantastic basketball player and an athlete. Johnny was smart, intelligent, and respectful, plus was always consistent with everything he did. For the both of them being consistent was very important and they lived by it. Johnny fully understood that it didn't matter how good you can play the game of basketball. Being a great ball player wasn't the key to college. Being educated, and graduating top of your class was what would take them there. He also accepted the fact that a scholarship was probably the only way that he and his brother could even go to college. They knew their mother could not afford to send them. She was already struggling with money living pay check to pay check. So with that being said Johnny would put 100% in all he would do. When it came time to weathering the storm, Johnny was the brother that had no problem with the bare minimum.

Their living condition wasn't the best but it also wasn't the worst. The way Johnny would act towards his mom was different from his brother. Now don't get me wrong, Ronny highly respected and loved his mother a whole lot, but Johnny was just a little more caring. He would not "smart mouth", suck his teeth or disobey her in anyway. He would never attempt to do anything that would hurt or upset her. His mother was his heart, his teacher, his everything. Now Ronny was pretty much the same except that he would spend a lot of time with a few kids around the way that his mom did not approve of. Ronny knew that hanging out with these friends worried her but that didn't stop him from doing so. His mother never blamed his friends for his action, not once. But she knew that his action had a lot to do with the people he hung out with. Ronny wasn't only book smart, he was also street smart. The drug business came to him naturally. Unlike Johnny, for him living with the bare minimum was not an option. Selling drugs wasn't something that he was proud of, it was something that he felt he had to do. He got sick and tired of hearing his mother cry herself to sleep almost every night. There was never enough money for the things they needed, never mind the things they wanted. Just that alone is enough stress for a fourteen year old kid to bare.

On their fifteenth birthday, Crystal decided to take them out for a nice lunch to spend some family time together. After eating, talking, and laughing she pulled them close to her and said to her boys "Happy Birthday. It seems like yesterday that I was holding the both of you in my arms. Now look at you! Almost all grown up right before my very eyes. It all happen so fast but I tell you, it has been one beautiful experience. Now listen to me. As you grow older and older life will become harder and harder so don't rush it. Let life come to you. In the beginning life will seem very long, but as you get closer to the end, it will start to seem very short. You can have any and everything you want in this world if you put your mind to it. You must believe and strive to reach that place you see yourself at in the future. Trust me you will reach every goal you set if you are determined. There are no barriers between you and success but there is a barrier between you and failure. It won't be an easy journey but it will be up to you to make it happen. It will take hard work, dedication, determination and faith. I say these words to you and hope that you take heed. I also know that your father's blood flows through the both of you. He was a great man and I need for the both of y'all to also be great men. What I have been wanting to tell you both is that I have been back and forth to the doctors for the past few months. I have been diagnosed with breast cancer and the doctor says I'm at a sixty present chance of living with a five to ten year cap, maybe even less, who knows. I have went for a second opinion, even a third but all of the doctors agree." Ronny and Johnny sat there in shock staring at their mom without blinking. Their eyes then turned red and watery as tears begin to pour down their faces. They quickly took hold of their mom squeezing and hugging her so tight without letting go for a very long time.

CHAPTER 3

The news had a very strong impact on Johnny. Ronny didn't take it too well either. He started staying out later than usual and making a lot more money than he usually made. The news of his mother's sickness really affected him. But, just as his grades decreased, his money increased. His reputation begin to grow. Ronny would sometimes have long talks with his brother about his view on life and why he was doing what he was doing. It was kept from their mom. Crystal had no idea what her son was up to.

One afternoon Crystal was doing laundry and went in the boy's closet to get the dirty cloths. As she pulled the basket, a sneaker box fell leaving bags of coke all around her feet. She stood there in shock! After gathering the box filled with drugs she brought it to her room. Crystal was so disappointed, she couldn't believe her eyes, as she sat there in her bedroom waiting for her kids to get home from school. She was contemplating on what to do and what to say. Shaking her head, tears pouring down her face she thought she could approach her son calmly.

But, as soon as they walked through the door, she picks up the box filled with drugs and throws it at Ronny. She slapped him in the face with so much force he stumbled back. Then she grabbed him by the shirt pulling him closer to her, screaming, yelling and crying, **"WHY?! WHY THIS?!"** After letting him go she placed her finger in his face and began to speak very slowly but stern. You listen to me and listen well. This type of lifestyle, I did not teach you. I raised y'all better than that and this is how you repay me? I know we are struggling, but I told y'all that you need to be strong! Ronny says "I am strong, and smart but I can't live life seeing you struggle like this, I just can't." "I'm very sorry mom but this is the only way I know how to help, so please let me help." Crystal says **"No!"** I told you to be smart, book smart, and strong mentally because they can hold you down, chain you up but they could never lock your mind. You listen really well. This kind of business may seem good in the beginning, but it's a disaster in the end. Listen baby, it's the same story everywhere dead or in jail. Just because the system doesn't change doesn't mean the people in it can't! So I need for you to smarten up and stick to the teachings that I've taught you, yes it might be hard in the beginning but it will be a blessing in the end. Now you choose because I will not allow this type of living under my roof.

Ronny then looks at her and said "a man that can't provide for his family isn't fully man until he can provide for his family." As he looks her straight in the face, breathing hard and says, "You're absolutely right about everything you said! But I'm willing to take that ride rather than sit here and watch you struggle." Ronny then packs his things, and there he was, on his way to Florida were the weather and the money was always good. Johnny stood there holding his mom as she cried her eyes out.

Watching her son turn his back on their family was another brick added to the stress wall. Jonny could not understand how his brother could be so smart and choose a path that was so stupid.

CHAPTER 4

Now, on his way down to Miami, he met a guy name Case. Case was on his way back to Miami from upstate New York. Case was short but stocky, dark skin complexion with a lazy eye, you could tell that he had no fear in his heart what so ever. Case was also worth a lot of money but you couldn't tell by the way he looked. Don't get me wrong Case stayed looking sharp he just would always keep it simple.

* * *

Case then introduced Ronny to a guy named Jay. Now, this might be the man you want to know about. Jay was the laid back one. He stood no taller than six two, light skin, fresh low cut, Cartier frames and button up shirts. Jay always had money on him and a thirty eight special that he kept with him at all times literally. He would even fall asleep with it, wake up with it, eat with it and even shit with it. The one thing he was about was business and protecting what was his. He wasn't the type to go and take something from another person he was the type to make something happen on his own. Young kid but he had the mind of an old head on a one way road to riches.

Now Jay and Case wasn't brothers but they were raised in the same house together. Jay was twenty one, and Case was twenty three, they were well known as if they lived a hundred years. Ronny was so much younger than them both but he spoke with so much humbleness they clicked just like that. They placed Ronny under their wing and taught him the good, and the bad. When he was around them he did more listening then talking, he would pick their brains every chance he got. Learning was something he loved no matter which way it came from, left, right, up or down he was like a sponge. He paid good attention and comprehended everything they taught him. He was by their side every second, minute an every hour of the day. He developed two times more knowledge than he already had. He also grew so much heart, bravery, loyalty, and respect. Jay later gave Ronny the name "Smooth", because he was so smooth in everything he did especially the way he treated the females. But Ronny wasn't a player he would keep his head on his shoulders at all times, and his other head in his pants. He learned at a very young age that these females will get you caught up, shot or robbed quick. He was definitely cut from a different cloth. When he heard the question being ask, "What percentage are you?" He said to himself, "the lower one." I quote Mr. Carter, "the percentage who don't understand is higher than the percentage who do, check yourself what percentage is you?" Now, with Smooth having the best of both worlds by being book and street smart, it was perfect for the game that he was ready to play. At times he would wonder about his mother and his brother, but his mind was made up and there was no turning back. He also would think about his best friend Steven that was serving a thirty year to life sentence at the age of fifteen. Steven was his best friend, they would hang out with each other every single day twenty-four seven and now, he will never see the outside of them walls again. So Ronny took time out of his day, every now and then to write him.

[LETTER 1.]

Dear Steve,

I don't know whether to blame you or the system that was set up for us to be in there. I believe we both have fallen victim because we will always be in jail, just out here you minus the bars. When the judge gave you thirty years to life he also gave it to the ones that love you too. Don't think that just because we are on the outside that we don't suffer along with you. Twenty four seven, three hundred sixty five days a year, don't a minute pass me by that you don't cross my mind. Whether you receive one letter or one hundred letters. Whether you receive one dollar, or one hundred dollars, our love for you don't change. But what keeps me pushing is I have learned and programed my mind to be strong mentally and I need for you to do the same thing. My mother was trying to teach me this for a long time and now I got it. Listen Steven, just because your life stopped out here don't mean that it don't continue in there, and at the same time are life don't stop it continues out here. Keep your head high and your mind strong never give up, life is what you make it. Ronny, aka Smooth.

CHAPTER 5

Meanwhile Johnny was home taking care of his mother. The breast cancer wasn't the only thing eating her alive. She cried her eyes out every single day for weeks at a time praying to God that her son will walk through them doors, but nothing. Week's turned into months, and months turned into years. Her prayer was not answer but she never gave up hope. She began blaming herself. Her heart was broke and she was filled with so much pain. She kept asking herself over and over again, "Why did I kick my child out? My own flesh and blood. Why?" Crystal could not forgive herself until Johnny finally said "enough!"

He took hold of his mother's hand, sat her down and said, "listen to me mom, you can't keep holding on to this. You're going to have a nervous break-down, or drive yourself insane. It's not your fault. You are not the one to blame. From day one all you ever did was bust your butt to give us all that you could. You probably wasn't able to give us everything that we wanted but you made sure that we had everything we needed. We were well taken care of, from a roof over our heads to having clothes on are backs and food in aur mouths. You gave us real unconditional love. You showed us what path to take in life and what path not to take. You made it so simple and so clear. It was like night and day. So please don't beat yourself up because you did your part. When I woke up early this morning before leaving the house, I made my bed and tonight I'm coming home to lay in it." I love my brother very much but when he made the choice to leave the house that day, he also made his bed and now he has to lay in it.

Crystal then hugged her son and squeezed him so tight crying and laughing at the same time in joy. She was so happy to hear those words coming from her young son's mouth, words of wisdom. Johnny loved his mother a whole lot and he appreciated everything his mother did or attempted to do for him and he also did his part. Every day after school he would get home and before doing anything else, he would do his chores. Afterwards he would do his homework then he would read for about an hour or two. After making sure his mother was all set and didn't need anything, he would go out with a few friends and play ball for a few hours then he would return home to spend the rest of his time taking good care of his mom. He was an amazing kid. Sometimes he would wonder about his older brother but he wouldn't stress it too much. He would take his mind off of a lot of things by exercising his body and his mind. His level of reading was off the charts. He loved to read, it was basically in his blood. His father, mother and brother were also readers, but the one thing that motivated Johnny to continue to read, was a statement that was made, recorded, and documented a very long time ago, it said, "If you want to hide something from a black person put it in a book." That quote made him think deeper than just the top layer of things. That was the reason he spent a lot of time in his deep thoughts contemplating about his surroundings, pondering on life itself. He had the mind of an adult at the age of fifteen. Johnny was still pushing for a full scholarship. That was number one on his list and giving up was not an option. The harder they made it for him in school the more he wanted it. His mother was his support. He wanted to make her proud of him. Johnny felt his mother deserved to see one of her sons succeed and giving her what she wanted was something he desired more than life itself. Crystal loved and appreciated her son more than words can explain. Johnny would always bring his mother something home on his way from school whether it was something small or big she would always appreciate it. But today was a special day, it was his moms thirty fifth birthday. So after school, he stopped by the store to pick up a card and a piece of her favorite cake. He couldn't wait to surprise her and see the smile on his mother's face. Johnny entered the house very quietly almost on his tippy toes trying not to make a sound. He pushes her bedroom door open very slowly then screams "Happy Birthday!" His heart dropped, the cake fell to the floor, his breathing stop, and his eyes open wide! He sees his mother on the floor. Dead! He runs over to her crying "No!!!" He drops to the floor and wraps his arms around her cold body rocking her back and forth.

Johnny was now officially traumatized! The only thing he had left in this world to hang on to was now gone forever. The month and day Crystal was born matched the month and day she died. With both parent's dead and his brother nowhere to be found, for the first time in his life he felt as if his back was now against the wall. He felt as if he had nobody to turn to. He kept all his hurt and frustration inside. It began to build up and at this very moment everything to him became pointless, even school! He felt as if he was forced to follow in his brother's footsteps and that's what he did.

CHAPTER 6

It was now four years later and Johnny was something wicked! Not only was he a hustler he became more like a monster. His trigger finger became itchy, his heart turned cold, no care and no fear at all. He had one goal and one goal only and that was to take, take, and Take! Until there wasn't any more to take even if it cost him his life. From time to time, he would still have these flash backs of his mother laying on the floor, and his brother walking out that door. These thoughts turned Johnny into a totally different person. His targets became two types of people. That was, those who had what he wanted, and those who got in the way of what he wanted and that was money. For a piece of paper to be so light it held a lot of weight. He had no care at all for anyone so much so that he would walk right up to a person an take them out, just like that! No love, no regret, no feeling at all. He enjoyed the action, fell in love with the streets, married the money and gave a fuck about life. To him killing became like second nature along with three other friends that felt exactly the same way. Their names were Brooks, Tray, and China. Johnny then went by the name "Streets."

Four kids dedicated to three things, and three things only. Money, Power, and Respect! They were playing for keeps with nothing to lose. Now with China being the only girl she was pretty handy with a gun. She wasn't a tomboy but, she was very aggressive for a girl and very beautiful. China was about five eight, carmel complexion, chinky eyes, with long dark hair. Besides that she was a cannon ball always ready to explode.

Brooks and Tray were cousins. Brooks was about six feet tall, dark skin, kind of skinny but ripped. Tray was about the same height, brown skin, and kind of husky with a mean mug. Now, Tray was wicked with the music he spent a lot of his free time writing music but flowing was his hobby, getting money was his job. One day Johnny asked a question "who's ready to take this to the next level?" China's hand was the first one up followed by the others.

Johnny smiled and said "Good!" Then our first mission starts with Flaco. China responded "who's Flaco?" Flaco was my brother Ronny's connection for his drugs. Ronny told me that this "Flaco guy" owns about seventeen houses in CT, and guess what? Sixteen of them are stash houses filled with cash. Every last one of their eyes lit up like lamps. Streets shook his head and said "yes." And just like Streets planned it, they hit Flaco's every day hang out. They kicked the door in then let off a full clip in the air. Then they told everybody to lay on their stomachs. Streets then said "Now that I have your full attention, my name is Streets." I'm going to ask a few questions and I'm going to need a few answers. Number one! Who's Flaco? All of a sudden a guy starts getting up and says "I'm him" what do you want from me? I bother no one, I pay my dudes, and I run my fucking operation with no problem, What do you want!? Streets says "I never thought you would ask." Streets then walks up to him in a very slow pace and said "your stash houses!" Then shoots Falco twice, once in each leg. Flaco drops to the floor screaming, cursing and yelling. Streets then says "Now I hope I have your full attention, you have less than ten seconds to write down all the addresses to your stash houses, and I mean all sixteen of them. If you still decide to play tough guy, I will sit here and torture every last one of you until I get what I want. Flaco then says "And if after all the torturing you still don't get what you want, and we decide to sit here and die one by one, then what?" "That won't happen" Streets replies, then Flaco says "And what makes you so positive?" Streets says "because you're the head, and what is the body without the head? Nothing!" Streets then places the barrel straight in his face and pulls the trigger. After blowing Flaco's brains all over the place, he then cocks the gun back and said in a loud tone "Next!".

Streets then said "We can make this easy or hard, we came for the money! Give it up or die very slowly." Someone then said in a loud voice "Is that what you want from us? Money? Are you crazy? Do you really think we are just going to let you come up in here flash a few guns, boss us around, and then take what we earned? You have to be insane." He then reaches for his gun as quick as possible but not fast enough China was standing over him with a forty four magnum and **BOOM** blew the side of his face clean off. Damn! That's a bad bitch! They then grabbed another guy by the shirt, tied him down to the chair and started to break his fingers one at a time. Then someone said "STOP!" Ok, its over you win. Streets then turned to look at the person who was talking, nodded his head up and down and said "OHHH, now you get it?" The guy said "Yes, it's over!" As he wrote down every address and handed it to Streets. As streets looked at it he said in a medium tone "Very, very smart, but very, very stupid". The guy said "why stupid?" China answered with a smirk on her face "Because we don't leave any witnesses!" Then Streets, China, Brooks and Tray put everybody out of their misery. Two shots, each to the face. Leaving them laying in puddles of blood they then lit a match and fled the scene.

They say money is the root of all evil but not in their case. Money was the root to their success. There was nothing evil about splitting over one million dollars in cash. It was like hitting the jackpot. This was only the beginning. They began to hit all the major drug dealers one after another and money began to pour in. They were on a mission to suck the streets dry and that's what they did. Streets knew how to play the game he was in. He also knew that the number one rule was loyalty to his friends, so he would split everything right down the middle. He closed all the cracks to any kind of jealousy, envy, or hate between them. He was a true entrepreneur. Streets was a different breed and this is why China fell in love with him so fast. China goes on to say "Now, before you judge me or look at me as a typical female who loves a guy with money, cars and jewelry please understand one thing, I am not a gold digger or a hoe. I'm a women that makes her own and has her own money. A man don't make me or break me. "She continue on saying, so why him right? Because I see the real him behind all the hurt, pain and anger. I see a lot deeper than what yall see. I see the intelligent side of him, the charming, the caring, and the loving. He makes me smile at times when all I want to do is cry. He makes love to my mind not only to my body. Strong and gentle at the same time. Sometimes he can be like hot fire, other times like cold winter. He is my everything. This is why I would never leave his side, and that is why I'm here now, until death do us part. "Someone once asked me a question, they said "how do you feel when you take another person's life?" I answered and said the feeling I get isn't good, it isn't bad either, but maybe someday that might change, until that day comes this is the life I'm in and this is the life I choose."

CHAPTER 7

S mooth receives a letter from Steven

[LETTER TWO].

> *Dear Ronny, reading your letter today didn't only put*
> *a smile on my face it also made me think. Think about*
> *things you said, then I started to ponder on days of slavery*
> *about the whole system and how we were stripped from*
> *are natural teachings then brain washed. Hear me out,*
> *back then they would chain us up and teach us only*
> *what they wanted us to learn, and feed us only what they*
> *wanted us to eat. Then I thought about now in the two*

thousands, they still chain us up and put us in jail, and teach us only what they want us to know, and feed us only what they want us to eat. Same shit different toilet. I was told by one of the OGs up here "the only difference between you and another person is the choice you make." And he was right. What I did to put myself in here was my choice. I been locked behind bars for over twelve years trying to move on and live with this regret in my heart, and it's been killing me. When you love someone it's a beautiful thing, but at the same time it can get really ugly. Love will have you trying to do the impossible just to make that someone you love happy, or even smile. But love will also grab your heart from every direction and rip it apart until happiness and smiling is not an option anymore. It's getting late, and almost time for lights out. Talk to you soon. Your friend Steven

CHAPTER 8

Now smooth was basically raised by Case and Jay, they became more like older brothers to him. They also knew that Smooth wasn't an ordinary kid. He was to unique, and different especially when it came to business. Smooth was a professional money maker in his own way. As time passed by, things started to grow, and money came in faster than they were able to count by hand. So they went out and bought money machines after purchasing a house. This house was strictly for counting money. Jay, Case and Smooth sold the purest cocaine you can find in Miami, the highest grade of weed there was. These guys moved drugs like no other, everything was in and out. They had the streets on smash and if anyone was to cross the line in anyway Jay wouldn't hesitate to get that person clipped. Case and Smooth didn't have a problem with blowing somebody's head clean off. They were well known around Miami and well respected. People looked up to them, they were almost like movie stars. It was almost impossible for the FBI to catch them with their hands dirty, being that they had hundreds of workers including a few cops on their payroll as well. They was about their money for real so they didn't party too much. If they did go out it was one or two places, and that was either a restaurant to discuss business, or a local bar to have a few drinks an shoot a little pool.

One night they all went out for dinner and talked about allowing Smooth to take over and become their number one man. While sitting there eating, Jay asked Smooth a question. He said "How long have we known you? "Smooth paused for a second, looks them straight in the face and says in a low voice "over thirteen, fourteen years." Jay then looked Smooth straight in the eyes repeating what smooth just said. "Thirteen, fourteen years huh" Blood sweat and tears you learned everything we have taught you. **You have even developed a high level of honesty, loyalty, and respect. You've mastered this way of living and survived it. Your light shines different than ours, and there is no one fit for this number one spot better than you. We will support you one hundred percent in everything you do from this day on.

Some people say that this was the smartest move that Jay and Case ever made, and it was. Being that Smooth was sharp and had the knowledge of a hustler. With a business mentality that was off the charts along with his father's blood running through his body, it was only natural for him to think big. He was all about investing his money and building his own. The mentality and thinking of Smooth was beyond deep. He would study and analyze everything until the rules of the streets became like a blue print in his head. Smooth was also careful with everything he did and in every move he made. People began to show more love and more respect than before. It was a beautiful thing, no problems, no beef what so ever. Smooth was laid back and always on point. He would keep one eye open at all times and his circle tight. Plus he took really good care of those around him, believe me when I say Smooth had it all mapped out. When he was asked "how are you able to maintain and keep everyone happy?" He replied "try throwing some crumbs to a group of birds and watch them fight" But throw a loaf of bread and watch them share." This world is all a game to them, they make it so there is not enough money to go around which then puts us in this survival state of mind. That's why we shoot at each other, rob and kill for the love of money, it's all political. Smooth knew that if he was going to take this to the next level it was either now or never. So he took a few steps back so that he can view himself from the outside looking in rather than the inside looking out, and his view was crystal clear. It was time for him to take it to the next level. Smooth had a master plan, all he needed was Jay an Case. Now there was one thing that Smooth took very serious and that was trust. He was not the kind of person to give it out twice to the same person, it was a one shot deal with him. Like they say, "first time shame on you, second time shame on me." Not with him, you didn't have to worry about that with Smooth he wasn't giving out that second chance not in this life. He was always two steps ahead of the person who thought they were two steps ahead of him. It's almost as if he mastered the thinking of Kunta Kenta, almost learning how to be a smart dummy if you know what I mean. When they start to realize we know too much we then become a threat. You see what they did to Malcom X and MLK right? Then use what they got to get what you want, but do it in silence. Pick their brains, study their every move and search for perfection. Now Smooth never got comfortable with those who claim to be his friend, he knew that this was a dirty game to be in, and that anything goes. He also knew in order to survive out here in this world you would have to be on your" A "game at all times. Never letting your guard down because in a blink of an eye you can get caught slipping, just one time and that's all it takes. Smooth was ready to turn it up a notch. So he called for a meeting with the five leaders from the major drug blocks in Miami an from that day on the game really changed. Smooth placed a duffle bag in front of every last one of them filled to the top with cash totaling over one million dollars apiece. They said "what is this for"? Smooth replied "this is for your loyalty, honesty, and respect" they all said "What?" we've known you for over ten years now, all we ever did was give you our respect. "Smooth said in a loud voice—NO! Yall feared us for the past ten years no real respect, no real loyalty or honesty at all. They all stood there very astonished. Smooth went on to say "plus I rather be respected then feared. Respect last longer than fear. When someone respects you they care for you, do for you, and love you all out of respect. But when someone fears you, their put in the middle of two things, and that's either be ruled by the thing they fear for the rest of their life, or kill that thing they fear so they can rule their self" "y'all don't look like the type that would want to be ruled by another human being and maybe the guys that work for y'all don't either. Maybe they don't even respect you rather they just fear you." Every last one of them approached and shook Smooth's hand making direct eye contact amazed at the way he just broke that down. Now I want for you to take this money and make a life time investment with your team. Start to take good care of them, help their families, pay them more than the amount they worked for and trust me then you will discover real honesty, loyalty, love, and respect forever. Try to avoid beef with others. Don't be the type of guys that goes around messing with other people's women that alone will get you killed. "Then watch how fast your money grows" if you keep everybody around you rich then nobody in your crew will ever go broke, because if everybody around you is rich they got your back. Sort of like a safety net I quote "If you hang around nine broke friends you're bound to be the tenth." Follow what I'm saying and you'll be successful. Jay and Case sat there the whole time but didn't open there mouths not once. They were even taken away by the wisdom and knowledge Smooth just dropped on them. Smooth just confirmed that they were in good hands so they supported him 100% in all that he did no matter what.

Smooth had plans to clean up his money so he started his own construction company and called it {Sharp and Smooth Designs}. Just as he planned all his drug money was washed and cleaned. Within one year his company started building clientele and receiving calls from people all over the place. I'm talking jobs worth millions. Smooth wasn't only cleaning his money he was now making clean money, and man did that feel good. The thing that really changed the game wasn't only starting this company, it was expanding it. One afternoon Smooth was in his office when five familiar faces in a respectful manner walked in. Smooth sat back and said "it's been a few years, what brings you back?" They said "what brought us back was you and the fact that you didn't ask for nothing in return, so in return we brought you a gift. "They dropped ten duffel bags on the floor of his office totaling more than twenty million dollars. Smooth then placed his hand on his face rubbing his cheek with his index finger, contemplating real deeply. Smooth then nodes his head and says "good job!" and I take that the money is for? They said "for your partnership." Smooth then says "so you mean to tell me that I came to you with the intention to give and not receive, and in return I receive that same loyalty, honesty, respect and on top of all that, twenty million dollar?" They all said "yes". Smooth looks them straight in the face with a smile, stands up shakes their hands firmly and says welcome aboard. Once again Smooth made a bigger investment.

CHAPTER 9

Smooth's job was to make sure that the material was ordered and delivered on time. Jay and Case would make sure that their crew was ready for unloading the shipment, breaking it down, weighing and bagging it up. Everyone else's job was to supply it in the streets. The way Smooth had it set up was perfect. It was a beautiful system and at this time the drug game was a beautiful business to be in especially when Jay's step father, owned acres and acres of the coco leaf and the highest quality of bud you could find. Everyone was happy and money started to pour in two to three times more than before, so much that they needed to hire people for counting and separating the money. They had built in cameras installed because when you're making this kind of money even when you give a person their fill they still want more. I like to use the word "Greed" so always on their Ps and Qs at all times. Now along with a privet jet that they had owned to transport their drugs they also used the car dealership that Case managed. They sold expensive cars, with zero miles and seats still with the plastic on them. Vehicles ranging from twenty to a hundred thousand dollars, being sold for thirty to forty percent off. Their clientele raised sky high, customers were happy and satisfied with the service they were getting, never any complaints. This brought in more money than they expected, and once again Smooth and his crew reach another level. Just like Biggie would say "sky is the limit." They increased by fifty percent of their last year salary which was over four hundred million dollars. It wasn't the cars they were worried about, these brand new vehicles were also being used for their drug trafficking on a weekly basis. Over five hundred cars were being loaded with tons of the purest cocaine you can find and the highest grade of weed on the face of the earth. These cars would be delivered to the back of the dealership with a crew already on standby, they would unload every single car within minutes into the back of these sixteen wheeler riggs. They will then take the drugs to their factory were everything operates twenty four hours a day. Jay looked at Smooth and said "I got one word for you, Genius. You're not only cut from a different cloth you are the cloth that others claim to be cut from. Congratulations your one of the chosen ones!"

CHAPTER 10

Streets did not only fall in love with the money he also fell in love with the action that brought him the money. He started taking everything from everybody, running up in houses tying people up shooting dogs even flipping over fish tanks. Extorting and black mailing, people feared him for the fact that he was willing to do anything at any giving time. Streets received some news that sent them on a vacation. He heard that Flaco's main drug connect is living mighty well out in Chicago. They all see one thing and one thing only "money!" Street said and guess what? He's not the middle man he's the man before the middle, and I'm not talking about the sixty million that we are worth now. No, I'm talking about over two hundred million dollars. They all looked at Streets with their eyes bigger then there heads, and China said "are you ready for a vacation baby?" and just that fast they were on the next plane.

Flying first class to Chicago, lounging, talking and laughing, eating then topping it off with a few shots of Grey Goose. Streets then reclined back kicking his feet up and said to them all "look at us, we have come a long way and it may not be the life we all dreamed that we would have, but it beats the life that we lived and had. Everything we have been through over the years will always be remembered. That is something we have to live with forever. The day we decided to take what didn't belong to us was the day we created enemies. This is a one way street that leads to two things, money or death. So as long as we are alive we will continue to take what doesn't belong to us, and protect what's ours even if it means our life. But our goal is to be successful not dead so be alert, and any sudden moves from anybody shoot first ask questions last. Now here's the plan when we touch down. We will lay low for a few weeks keep our ears to the streets until we figure out who is who and what is what. We might have a lot of money, a lot of guns and a whole lot of power but "the strong move silent, the weak start riots."{Thanks to Bleek} Streets then said "now listen up this job is a little different then back home, we have to put thought into this, plan it out then attack, trust me easy money for us all, you'll thank me later."

So they stayed in a suite at the casino for a few days. The first night they did some gambling, few clubs and a nice restaurant but nothing too fancy. They came for one reason and one reason only, an that was for Chino! So Streets began planning and master minding the whole thing and it didn't take no longer then forty eight hours to do so.

CHAPTER 11

China begins following this women to her car but the women starts to feel that she's being followed and starts to speed up a little. She then glances over her shoulder and sees that China also picked up speed. She then takes off running towards her car, China takes off running after her. Scared for her life she unlocks her car jumps in and quickly locks the doors and before she can turn the key she hears a gun go click, click from the back seat, a man's voice says "don't even do it" she froze in her seat and said in a crying voice "please don't hurt me" Streets then said "don't worry I'm not going to hurt you." He then open the door for China, she got into the passenger seat and they then had the lady drive them to her house. When they got there they forced the women through the door pushing her on the living room floor were her seven year old son was tied up along with her husband Chino. The boy was fine but Chino had a few cuts and bruises being that he tried to put up a fight but didn't get too far. Tray and Brooks had kept it all under control. Chino yells out at them saying "what is it you want from us?" Cause if its money you got the wrong people. Streets says "nah we have the right people", he then throws some pictures on the floor of Flaco and his crew with their brains blown out from the back of their heads. Cocks his gun back and points it straight at the little boy, Chino says "whatever happen to not harming the women or the children?" Streets then said "they're not harmed, well at least not yet". But! if you don't give up everything that I came for then yes they will be harmed, and yes they will be killed. Chino says "it's in the kitchen underneath the floor take it all and leave us the hell alone you son of a bitch." Tray, Brooks and China head to the kitchen and lifts the floor up finding clean cut green bills compressed in plastic Chino says a second time "Take it and go! Please!! My son is scared to death and my wife is crying her eyes out." "There's over five million dollars there," Chino said "are you satisfy?" Streets looked him in the face for a long time without blinking and said "yes I'm satisfied just not a hundred percent!" Chino then says "what else do you want from us we have nothing!" Streets said "I want it all!" Then points the gun at his wife's head and says "I want the money that you and your wife have been stashing in the bank for the past ten years." China, Tray, and Brooks eyes lit up, they were even surprised to hear about that. Chino's wife starts crying and says to her husband "just give them what they want!" he yells at his wife telling her to shut her mouth, and then says to them "I have no clue what you are talking about!" Streets pulls the gun away from Chinos wife and shoves it in his mouth. Streets said "you mean to tell me you are willing to risk the lives of you family over a few dollars?" Chino says "a few dollars?" "I worked hard for that money I been through hell and back and I'm supposed to just hand it over just like that? You and your crew could go to hell" then spits in Street's face. China then runs over to Chino and pistol wiped him in the face leaving his lip busted wide open. Chino's wife cry's out "stop please I'll do anything just promise not to hurt us." Streets replied "any other time I wouldn't do this but in this case I promise". You give me want I want, and you will get what you want. She asks "what is it you want? Streets said "I need for you to clean out your account including safety deposit boxes with in the next twenty four hours." She said "are you kidding me that's a bank we are talking about, you can't just withdraw that amount of money including safety deposit boxes without someone asking questions, it's just impossible!" He then looked at her, nodded his head up and down and said "yup, you are one hundred percent right but that's if we do it your way" she looked at him with a straight face and said "what do you mean?" Streets said "were not making a withdrawal. You're going to help us leave that bank with it all. Emptying out your accounts and safety deposit boxes. Then we will disappear leaving you and your family harmless with enough money for y'all to disappear. You will never have to worry about seeing these four faces again in your life and that's my word. Now, here's how it will happen. You will go to work just as you would any other day, but this time you will be armed with a gun. Tray and Brooks will remain here with your husband and son until you, China and I return. Any false moves from you they're dead!"

CHAPTER 12

Early the next morning Jennifer walks into work calm and relaxed like any other day, clocks in then heads straight to her station. As time gets closer and closer she becomes nervous. Then she starts to think that one of her colleagues may have seen the gun. For the fact she kept looking over at her.

A few minutes later she starts walking towards her. Jennifer says to herself "if she says anything, about anything, I will not hesitate to blow her head clean off." As she gets closer Jennifer's stomach starts to knot up and her heart drops. Her mouth becomes very dry. But her hand wasn't too far from that pistol on her waist.

Her friend approaches her saying "How you doing today? You look a little under the weather are you ok?" Jennifer exhales out that deep breath she was holding in and said "oh yes, I'm fine just a little tired that's all, but thanks for asking." Her coworker said "you're welcome" then walked away, and just as Jennifer looks up she sees Streets and China entering the bank with their guns drawn.

Jennifer pulls out and tells all the bank tellers to back up against the wall then shoots one of them in the leg just to let the others know she wasn't joking. She then made them sit down with their arms behind their backs then zip ties their hands together. China made sure that everyone else was under control while Streets and Jennifer cleaned out everything that Chino owned. Not touching a single dollar from the bank's money just as he planned. He robbed Chino for every dime he was worth. Everybody got exactly what he promised and then they disappeared. This time they really hit the jackpot for real! They were worth over three hundred million dollars, Streets looked at them with a smile and said "now it's time for a real vacation, where is it going to be?" Tray looked at him and said "Miami," Streets said "Miami it is". On their way there China had a talk with Streets. China says to him. "Now that we have enough to retire, lets buy a house and finally relax like a real vacation" Streets felt as if he owed this to her being that she's been by his side from day one, so he kisses her an says "Yes China we are retiring, I promise and you can have whatever you want."

CHAPTER 13

[S mooth]
Now with all that has been going on Smooth still found time to write his friend.

[Letter 3]

Dear Steven,

A lot has happen within the past few years, too much to cover in this letter all at once. I think it's about time I come up and see you, we both have a lot to catch up on. But besides that there was something else I wanted to share with you. Just the other day I was reading and came across something very shocking. It said that ninety percent of those arrested and charged are innocent, but the fact that they do not have any knowledge of the law or fully understand their rights they all end up doing time in jail or on probation. Not realizing that even without a lawyer if they were to take it to trial they will still have a seventy to a seventy five percent chance of beating the whole case. So by keeping that kind of information from us allows them to keep their jobs. Why do you think they took the library out of the prisons? The same reason why they didn't allow slaves to read, and still till this day they are afraid of the strength and power that we have within us. For the system to be designed that way and followed for years is the worst thing ever, but in their eyes it was the best thing they ever did. It has gotten to the point where I don't know whether to put the blame on us for continuing to fall victim to the system, or blame them for creating it. What they have done to us is the worse crime you can ever do to someone. They took away our history and told "his-

story" and they completely brain washed our minds into

thinking that we are not capable of achieving anything.

What's sad is that we began to believe that, so we settle for

less. A very good friend of mine once said "of course you

can catch a nigga if you push him in a trap, and modern

day slave catchers look better with a badge" and he wasn't

lying. Listen Steven I know that you are going through a

lot right now because I can feel it when I'm reading your

letters, and holding it in may feel like the best thing at

times but it's the worst thing ever. Free yourself, read your

books and express how you feel on paper. Do whatever

you need to, to keep your mind right! The other day I

was reading your last letter you sent me and it made me

think real deeply about life, and how fast it passes you by.

I learned not to dwell to much even on the present time,

because just as you say now, it's already then, and before

you say later, it's already now. Life is only what you make it. I am no longer afraid to fail because I'm searching for perfection, feeling like the sky is the limit. Not caring about what others may think of me or say because if they don't love me for who I am, I rather them hate me for who I'm not. Well I'm going to end this letter by saying: keep your head high and stay strong, it isn't the end of the world your life still goes on. See you this week. Ronny aka Smooth.

[Letter 4]

Dear Ronny,

I hope this letter reaches you in time before you try to come up here to see me. The last visit I received was from my mother a few years back and since then I have rejected every visit. By me not seeing anyone really helps me get through the years, it allows me to focus on what's in here rather than what's out there. So please don't waste your time. The letters and the money you send me is more than

enough. Thank you so much for being a real friend and I

hope to hear back from you soon. Love Steven.

But the letter did not reach him in time. So there he was on his way up to go see his friend Steven. Upon arriving he had to walk through about four gates and be escorted by a correctional officer, he was then patted down and searched for drugs and weapons. After signing in he then takes a seat and waits for his name to be called. But every-ones name was called excepted his. The correctional officer approaches him and says "I'm sorry sir but Steven Patterson refuses to accept visits, he has for the past two years now. But Ronny insisted on seeing him, he asked the correctional officer to allow Steven to know it's his friend Ronny here to see him and he won't reject the visit, please. So the correctional officer said "wait here I'll be back" when he returned he approached

Ronny by saying "I told you so, but I think he knew you were coming he ask me to give this to you, it was a letter. He reached out and grabbed it as he sat down and began to read it, it said.

Hello Ronny, I kind of knew you still would come so I prepared this letter for you. Being that it will be impossible to explain this to you face to face. The pain that I live with every day the hurt that eats me up in the inside, you will never feel or fully understand unless it literally happen to you. Let me explain something to you, every morning I wake up at the same time, eat at the same time, rec at the same time, shower at the same time, then right back to sleep at the same damn time! Not because I want to but because I have to, at the end of the day it was me who had a choice to make and I made it. I want you to listen to me very closely. When someone continues to hurt something that you love very much over and over and over again there's only so much that you can take until you break. Day after day and night after night placing my hands over my ears wasn't working anymore the noise became louder and seemed as if it was getting closer and closer. All the yelling the screaming, cursing and hitting became normal to my mom but never to me. It was one day after dark when suddenly I was awaken by some loud noise and glass breaking. I quickly jumped out of my bed to see what was going on. I ran to my mom's room and found her boyfriend on top of her with one hand around her neck choking her and the other hand striking her in the face repeatedly one hit after another. My mom couldn't breathe, blood all over the place, I quickly ran over jumping on his back hitting him in the face, yelling and screaming "get off of my mother, stop!" finely he lets her go. My mom spitting up saliva and blood was all over the floor. He then swings me off of him causing me to slam right into the wall hitting my head. I got up and rushed straight to the closet and grab a twenty two pistol, the only thing that can save me and my mom's life at this very moment. But when Jason seen the gun pointed at him he froze and stood there breathing very hard. I then yelled "look what you did to my mom, look at her face and you call that love?" That isn't love that isn't love at all that's more like dislike and hate, but tonight you're going to pay for everything you put her through. My mother screams out "no baby please don't do it, it's not worth it put the gun down please." but as tears poured down my face, and my heart started to race, the gun shaking in my hand I then said to my mom "this is the true meaning of love I am willing to give up the rest of my life, so that you can live the rest of yours." Then looked him straight in the face and shot him five times in the chest and watched as he dropped to the floor. I stood there staring at my mom as I heard the sirens getting closer and the only thing that was running through my mind was I wanted her to be free. Free of hurt, pain, and abuse I wanted her to live in peace. To find true love, love that has meaning and action behind it, love that doesn't hurt, instead it feels so good. I wanted my mom to know what it's like to really have someone love her back. But on July 7, 2007, I received a visit from my mom, the most important person in my life. The moment she looked at me tears just filled her eyes. She said "I'm crying because of you." You sacrificed your entire life for me but love won't let me be free like you wanted, love won't let me leave and no matter how hard I tried to force myself away from him love pulls me right back to him. What I'm trying to tell you is I never left him, and I'm sorry. My breathing stopped, my stomach dropped, and it became very hard to swallow. My eyes filled with tears sitting there in shock, hurt and confused. At this very moment for the first time in my life, I felt as if I had died twice! How can my mother love another person more than me? I'm her child, where is the connection? Where's the love? I can't go on like this any longer. Living with this pain in my heart, this thought in my mind, it's nothing but torture. Then on top of that, being behind bars, it just puts me over the edge. This place doesn't transform a person from bad to good, instead it makes you worse. Your thinking starts to change your thoughts become deeper and more evil, everybody that you ever known, seen, or touched now only exist in your mind, no longer physical form. This is what prison does to you but I'm getting off this train, there's nothing here in this life for me, please don't think any less of me, I just can't fight this pain anymore, I'm done! See you on the other side . . .

LOVE YOUR FRIEND STEVEN . . . .

Smooth throws the paper down yelling, and screaming to the C/O **"There's something wrong with him!**

HURRY, pleases go help him, PLEASE!" a few officers rushed up to Stevens cell block to find him hanging by the neck. Steven Patterson was now deceased.

CHAPTER 14

A few days later they allowed Smooth, Case and Jay to attend his funeral. It was a very sad day for them, and it was also a thinking moment for Smooth. Yes he took it hard but he didn't act out, he had total control of himself, sat there so calm and relaxed. He thought to himself "if I go around hating the world and everything in it because of the loss of my friend, then I'm no better than the devil himself, and later I will still have to deal with the consequence of my actions and Steve will still be gone". At this very moment he stopped, took a few steps back looked at himself and said "How do I want to be remembered? Surrounded by violence, drugs, betrayal, is that what I really want?" "No I don't" Smooth was now outside the box looking in, and his vision was completely different. He seen a clear path to success and true success is not to destroy your people, it's to help them.

Smooth calls Jay and Case and has them gather everyone together for a meeting. Smooth stands up to make sure he has every-ones attention. He says, "first let me thank you all for being here I really appreciate it." The reason for this meeting most of y'all may not agree in the beginning, but hear me out to the end. I want for us to make the transition from the streets to offices, illegal to legit, ghetto to professional. Someone says "now hold up a minute, your telling me that you want us to give up a multi-million dollar drug business for an office?" Smooth shakes his head and says "yes" but not only an office, for the future, for the better, for us, our children and grandchildren. For a life time investment. Yes we might be giving up a multi-million dollar drug business but this business can't be passed down to our kids. It's not legit nothings legal, no paystubs, w2s, no ownership what so ever. We have been doing more harm to them than good, so it's time we change. We are caught between love and hate, we love the fact that this type of business brings us lots of money but hate the fact that we have to sell it to our own people destroying families by the thousands. It's either, we stand together the right way, or die together the wrong way. All it took was one person to stand and acknowledge him, then every last one of them stood up walked over shook his hand . . . . . Someone then said "so what is it we are doing?" Smooth said "what we do best, make money!

So from that day on they never sold another drug in their life. They went 100% legit and took Smooths Construction Company to a whole other level. Totaling over a thousand or so people that worked with them. Smooth spent more than twenty seven million dollar and paid for each and every one of them to go to trade school and in the matter of one year they all graduated and a few years later they became licensed professionals. S.S.D became the biggest construction company in Miami. They specialized in plumbing, pipefitting, welding, electrical, HVAC, automotive and more, you name it they have it. They built their own headquarters. They made it so they did not have to rent any machines or equipment instead they brought everything they needed. Just as he planned this company went through the roof. Money started to increase by the millions and growing by the months. Smooth ran this company to its largest and highest point, his M.O never changed "think big, win big."

Everybody was so happy enjoying the good life, teaching their kids and taking care of their family without going back and forth to jail and this was only the beginning. Smooth taught his friends and partners that the path that was laid out for us to take only leads to drugs, violence, prison, failure, and most likely dead before you reach your twenty's. But just because a path was laid out for you doesn't mean you have to take it. We now are creating our own path. It's not rocket science to see that our children are being designed and prepared to become the workers for their children. Ponder on this for a second . . . We were given drugs and guns by them, right?? Well the same ones who give it, take it away leaving us dead or doing time. And if they decide to release us it's with two things probation or a felony which is a stamp that prevents people who want to change unable to because no one will hire them. So what does that lead you back to? When there is no way to take care of your responsibilities, at that time it leads you back to what makes sense and enough cents make dollars. Then our kids follow in that same system, it's a never ending cycle. But by us no longer selling drugs it decreases the prison rate and increases the success rate. Then watch how the tables turn. Pay attention now. These people that spend billions and billions of dollars on sending their kids to school banking on the fact that we will become criminals securing their jobs. I want you to remember one important fact and that's America is not a country it's a business and those who sit up high and control us like puppets don't like it one bit. So the only thing we can do is to continue to build our own businesses and managing them ourselves. They don't care if your rich they just don't want us to own shit! Now that we own our own construction company and have created jobs lets continue. I'm talking let's not only build homes lets build casinos, hotels, restaurants, big investments.

They began to grow bigger and bigger, and went worldwide! They went from millionaires to billionaires which they made happen with hard work, dedication an determination.

CHAPTER 15

A few days later Smooth, Jay and Case got together for lunch in the cafeteria at their headquarters. They both wanted to tell Smooth how proud they were of him and how thankful they are. Being that S.S.D hasn't only changed their lives, it also has changed the lives of others. Smooth told them that they are very welcome and he loves them a lot. While sitting and chatting Smooth happens to glance over across the room and makes eye contact with this very beautiful women. He then smiles at her and she smiles back. Smooth gets up and makes his way over, as he approaches her table she stood up and shook his hand introducing herself.

"Hello my name is Amanda and yours," he said "pretty name, my name is Smooth." She smile and said you mean "Ron?" He looked at her very strange and said "excuse me?" She said "you don't know me but I know you". "How?" "I'm one of the attorneys at the law office that handles S.S.D Construction." Smooth replies, "oh ok, so then it's safe to assume you'd be interested in joining me for dinner tonight?" Amanda answered by saying "I was hoping you would ask." "8:00?" "Perfect!"

As Smooth walks to his truck he smiles, thinking how great life was and how better it could be if this women was the piece he didn't even realize was missing from his puzzle. Amanda had him thinking different possibly even building the family life . . . . . but then flash backs started to race through his head. He said to himself "all the money that I have don't erase the fact that I walked out on my family and that my mom had breast cancer and she needed me the most. I wish I could just hug her and say "I love you one last time, I wish that I can look my brother straight in the face and tell him "I got you little bro were going to be alright." But instead I was being selfish I might be successful now but I walked out on my family to get it. He then looked up at the sky and said "Johnny where ever you are in the world I want you to know that I'm sorry and I love you and if you're dead I pray to God that he be "just" with you being that he's a "just" ruler and if you're alive I pray that he allows me to feel and hear the sound of your heartbeat one last time, I love you man.

CHAPTER 16

[Streets] So there they were big blue skies, fluffy white clouds, crystal clear water and beautiful days in the sun, couldn't ask for anything better, Miami was the place to be. They stayed in a hotel right on the beach while China searched for a house she wanted. Things really got crazy when Streets hears the story about a ex-drug dealer who gave up a million-dollar drug business for a construction company. He then kept his ear to the streets doing what he does best. He gathered all the info that he needed to mastermind this plan. Even though Streets made that promise, he just couldn't keep it. So when he told the others what he was thinking they weren't too happy, especially China! He told them "we have to do this heist one last time! You don't even understand the amount of paper we can wipe our ass wit, I'm talking crazy figures. I swear we do this we will be set forever! I need y'all with me on this one, don't back out on me now! This will be it I swear," China looks at him shaking her head, "No! Leave it alone we have enough, we're already set, let's just stop, please let it go." Streets said. "what ever happen to death do us part?" China said. "Now you listen to me, I stuck by your side for over ten years and not once did I ever say no to a job. But there comes a time when enough is enough, BUT! If this is something you really want to do then I will do it this one last time and then I'm done, all of us are forever, and if you go back on your promise, I promise to leave you and believe me when I say, I won't go back on my promise!"

CHAPTER 17

[S mooth] Now the key to how Smooth got to where he's at now was First—Learning how to live with his regrets.

Second—Seeing others make mistakes and learning from his own.

Third—Thinking twice before he would talk and react and Last-Paying good attention, and following good advice. He was the type of guy someone would want to run their company, Smooth was the definition of an example for "true success."

It was 7am when Smooth was in his office chair reclining back looking out the window of his own company. He then said to himself "I really did it, I took the block and turned them into offices, I took the drug hustle and turned construction into my hustle, I did it and I'm real proud of myself." There was then a knock on the door, Smooth said "Come in" in walks Jay and Case, they sat down and chatted a little.

{The phone rang} Smooth picks it up and says "hello" his secretary responded "your 9:00 appointment is here" Smooth said "Thanks, can you please send them up." As the couple entered the room Smooth introduced himself and said please, take a seat. These are my assistants, as he looks over to Case and Jay. Smooth said "so how may I help you?" My wife and I were looking to buy a home out here in Miami. My wife can't seem to find a house she likes, so I thought we would come to you since I have heard nothing but good things about this company. I want her to create and for you to build exactly what she wants. Smooth says "Sounds great, then that's exactly what we will do." Before we get started I would like to go over some paperwork and a few questions. Streets interrupted him and said "one more thing I wanted to ask, is it true that you gave up over a million dollar drug business and started this company?" Smooth says "yes it is true" China says "WOW, that's an amazing story, just sounds too good to be true." At that time Brooks and Tray walks in the office with their guns drawn. Everybody then pulls out including Jay, Case and Smooth. Guns pointed at one another everybody ready to shoot. Smooth says "you're about to make a big mistake, this is a legit business, we have licensed firearms and been completely out of the drug business for years." Streets don't believe it, he then says "oh no, this is no mistake, every drug dealer finds a way to clean their money and this company is your cleanup! I want it all every fuckin dollar give it up or die!" Jay seen one of them about to pull the trigger so he let off a shot then they all fired at each other jumping behind chairs, desks and tables. Jay then hits Tray with a head shoot, bullet goes in and out of his face. Case then gets hit like three times in the chest falls flat on his back coughing up blood. Jay gets shot in the arm and ducks for cover still firing his gun. Streets get shot in the leg and falls to the floor, Smooth shot Brooks in the neck he dies instantly. China shot Jay in the chest, Smooth then shoots China in the hand she dropped the gun and ran out the door bleeding. Streets then let off some more shots just missing Smooth's head. Smooth falls to the floor the both of them out of breath, breathing hard Streets standing over him with his gun pointed straight in his face "don't make me do this" he said. "All you have to do is give me what I want and you'll live, it's as simple as that or you can play dumb and tuff guy and die for it. **Come on you know the rules to this shit, Once you're in your in, there's no getting out EVER."**

But as Streets began to look closer at this man, he then freezes for a second because he sees something in Smooths eyes that he only sees when he looks in the mirror, as if he knew this guy all his life, but the one thing you learn in these streets is instinct and on battle field hesitation can cause you your life! "Before streets can say **Ronny!**" Two shots into his chest, Smooth shoot him. Streets dropped the gun and fell to the floor holding his chest, Smooth gets up and walks over to him standing over his body gun pointed at his face, watching him die slowly. As Streets laid there coughing up blood he was trying to say something, almost like a name, and all of a sudden Smooth hears "Ronny, Ronny is that you?"

Smooths eyes widened and his heart stops, the gun falls and Smooth drops to his knees crying. He grabs Streets by the shirt and placing his head on his legs and says with a low voice "Johnny is that you?" In the middle of his shallow breaths is able to say "yes" Ronny then screams out **"Noooooo". This can't be, not this, NO GOD PLEASE!!!!!"** Johnny then dies right in his brothers arms and Ronny screams out even louder **"NOOOOOO."** He then jumps up, races outside, jumps into his car slams his foot on the gas causing the tires to burn out, speed begins to pick up very fast, swerving in and out of traffic, one hand on the wheel, music blasting loud! One hundred, one hundred an ten, one hundred and twenty miles per hour, car starts to shake, hard to control tears pouring down his face, car spins out flipping over four or five times with car parts and glass flying everywhere slamming into an embankment leaving the car upside down, people slamming on their brakes throwing their cars in park rushing over to see if he's ok . . . some people screaming he's dead, some screaming he's alive, but as they pull him out of the car they find him . . . .

TO BE CONTINUED . . .

ABOUT THE AUTHOR

My name is Deivone Tanksley. I come from New Britain, Connecticut. Subjected to living in the projects a small place called Mont Pleasant. Growing up I was surrounded by drugs, guns and violence so much so that it was normal to see needles laying on the ground even hearing gun shots in the middle of the day. With my mother struggling and my dad in and out of prison things around the house didn't go so well. I would keep all my thoughts and anger to myself. I would act out in school until I was kicked out and finally expelled from every school in New Britain. I was then sent to a school in Newington, called Newington Children's Medical Center where they were allowed to use physical restraint. Being there didn't change my behavior one bit. At the age of eleven I found myself locked up for the very first time. Just like they say "once you're in the system you're in." From that day on I continued in an out of Juvenile Detention until being sent to a Placement Home when I turned fifteen. Seventeen I was in long lain Youth Facility. Eighteen MYI and at Twenty I was in Northing CI, I have spent over ten years of my life in and out a lock up. In the year of 2006 I did the only thing that separates one human being from another and that was I made a choice, I chose to put myself and my family first rather than the streets an my friends. I then enrolled in trade school and 18 months later graduated with an electrical diploma. For the first time in my life I accomplished something good. I was now able to provide for my kids they right way, I father four children 3 boys and a girl. Growing up I would always write, from raps to poetry. It allowed me to express myself in another way rather than talk, you could say it was my outlet from life. Until about a year ago I decided to take my writing ability and put it in something other than just my thoughts. I chose to write a book. To create something powerful and to establish my presence in my absence. To also give hope to those that have been through similar upbringings like myself, to let the world know no matter where life takes you there's always a way out. All you have to do is be determined, dedicated and consistent. So whether my book sell one copy or a million copies, change one heart or a million hearts I have succeeded and reached my goal. There is and there will be a next generation and its starting with me . . .

CPSIA information can be obtained at www.ICGtesting.com
Printed in the USA
LVOW13s1253010414

379825LV00003B/764/P